Holly Keller

HENRY'S HAPPY BIRTHDAY

 Julia MacRae Books

A DIVISION OF WALKER BOOKS

First published in the USA 1990
by Greenwillow Books
First published in Great Britain 1990
by Julia MacRae Books
A division of Walker Books Ltd
87 Vauxhall Walk
London SE11 5HJ

Printed in Hong Kong by Imago

British Cataloguing in Publication Data
Keller, Holly
    Henry's happy birthday.
    I. Title
    813.54 [J]

ISBN 0-86203-474-4

For JESSE

"Wake up, Henry," Papa whispered.
"Today is your big day."

Henry jumped out of bed and stuck his feet into his slippers. He cleared his throat and started to sing. "Happy birthday to me, Happy birthday to me..."

Mama was in the kitchen putting the
icing on Henry's cake.
"Come and see," she called when she
heard him coming down the stairs.
"You said I could have chocolate," Henry
said when he saw it.

"Vanilla will be better," said Mama, and she spread the
last bit on the top. "Not everybody likes chocolate."
Henry made a face. "I do," he said. "And besides,
vanilla will be too plain."

Henry didn't want his cereal, so he followed
Mama into the dining room to set the table.

"Uh-oh," Mama said when she counted the sweet
baskets. "We forgot about Cousin Gertie.
Be a good boy, Henry, and give her yours.
I'll put your sweets in a paper cup."

Henry picked up the shiny, silver-coloured basket
and moved it slowly over to Gertie's place.
"What if you forget?" Henry said.
"Don't be silly, Henry. I won't."

When it was time to get dressed, Henry put on
his favourite T-shirt and his new sneakers.
He combed his hair and bounded back into
the dining room. "I'm ready," he announced.

"No, no," Mama said, and she laughed.
"Not today, Henry. Everyone else will be
wearing party clothes."

Henry buttoned his white shirt, and Mama
tied his bow tie.
"There," she said. "<u>Now</u> you are ready."

"I look stupid," he said sadly.

The doorbell rang, and Henry ran to answer it.
It was Aunt Sue and Cousin Gertie.

Aunt Sue gave Henry a big birthday kiss
that left a sticky red mark on his face.

Gertie gave him a very little package
wrapped in paper Henry thought was ugly,
and he knew it couldn't be anything good.

Henry's best friend, Mark, brought a big yellow box, but Henry could tell from the shape that it wasn't the thing Mark had promised.

And Timmy had left his present at home.

When everyone was there, Papa started the games.

Molly stuck a tail on Henry's back,
and Gertie called him a donkey.

The prize for musical
chairs was a little silver whistle,
and Henry wanted it.

But Timmy pushed him off the last chair just
as the music stopped. Henry was miserable.
"No more games," he said.

So Mama brought in the cake. Everyone sang "Happy Birthday" and Aunt Sue lit the candles. "One for each year and one to wish on," she said cheerfully.

Henry closed his eyes and blew. I wish, he thought,
that this were someone else's birthday.
And he tried hard not to cry.

Then Papa appeared with helium balloons and
a special party hat for Henry that looked
like a crown. Everyone clapped.

Mama cut the cake and Henry got the first piece.
It was pink and white inside with real whipped cream
between the layers. Henry took a bite. It was good.
"Not too plain?" Mama asked.
Henry shook his head.

When Henry opened his presents, he got a kite
and a set of paints with a dinosaur colouring book.

Mark really did get him the crocodile raft he had promised — it just had to be blown up.

Gertie's present was a tiny model fire
engine with a siren that really worked,
and Henry loved it.

When everyone had gone home, Henry sat on Mama's lap. "Was it a nice party, after all?" Mama asked. Henry nodded his head. "But I didn't make a very good birthday wish," he said.

Mama gave him a hug. "Never mind," she said.
"You have a whole year to think of another one."
Henry smiled. "OK," he said, "I will."